ISBN: 9781731134998

Published by Civin Media Relations
www.civinmediarelations.com

Printed in the United States

# <u>Dedication</u>

"In the end  we will remember not the words of our enemies, but the silence of our friends."

~ Martin Luther King

This book is dedicated to all the children of the world.

You alone possess the courage you need.

Just look within.

You will find it.

It's important to define courage,
In a manner that is clear.
It's not the one who's not afraid,
But the one who conquers fear.

*Courage for Charlie*

So here's the story of Charlie,
Who's best friend Matthew lives next door.
The two became the best of friends,
With the whole world to explore.

The boys would play from early morning,
Until the street lights came out at night.
Rode bikes, built tents, played video games,
Told ghost stories with bright flashlights.

Matthew was the athlete,
While Charlie played chess.
Matthew played what Charlie liked,
So Charlie could taste success.

Charlie knew his shortcomings,
With Matthew big and strong.
He was grateful that Matthew remained his friend,
And let Charlie tag along.

When the boys became teenagers,
On the first day of junior high.
Charlie waited to ride bikes to school,
But instead saw Matthew's bus drive by.

Matthew made the football team,
He loved to hear the cheers.
He started to exclude Charlie,
Getting pressure from his peers.

When he got home from practice,
He no longer hung out after school.
He simply waved to Charlie,
since Charlie wasn't cool.

One morning after class,
As Matthew walked through the door.
He saw a group of eighth graders,
Knock Charlie to the floor.

Charlie looked up at his friend,
Who didn't know what to say.
Charlie's eye caught Matthew's,
As he turned and walked away.

The boys walked home from school,
With sadness on their faces.
Though their houses still stood side by side,
They were in very different places.

Matthew sat at the dinner table,
But couldn't eat a bite.
His mother asked about his day,
She knew something wasn't right.

Matthew told his mother,
Why he lost his appetite.
She said he needed courage,
To stand up for what's right.

"You and Charlie are longtime friends,
So you need to make a choice.
You don't need to fight physically,
But you need to use your voice."

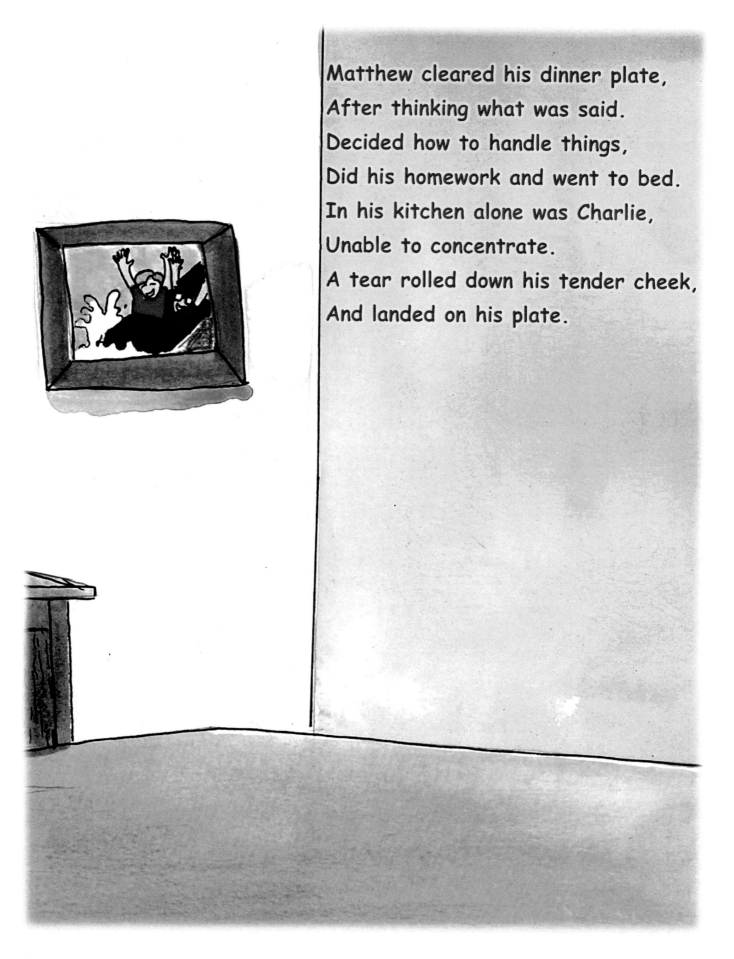

Matthew cleared his dinner plate,
After thinking what was said.
Decided how to handle things,
Did his homework and went to bed.
In his kitchen alone was Charlie,
Unable to concentrate.
A tear rolled down his tender cheek,
And landed on his plate.

The boys arrived to school the next day,
And history was repeated.
Matthew saw Charlie trying to defend himself,
But was about to be defeated.

*Courage for Charlie*

"STOP, he's my friend" said Matthew.
"He's no different than me or you.
If you want to be friends with me,
Be friends with Charlie, too."

Matthew helped Charlie to his feet,
As his teammates gave him looks.
He brushed off Charlie, who smiled at him,
And helped pick up his books.

The players made a plan that evening,
There was a knock on Charlie's door.
They had a favor to ask of him,
"Could Charlie keep the score?"

Charlie looked at Matthew,
With a smile full of rejoice.
See what happens his mother said,
"When you learn to use your voice?"

Charlie boarded the bus in the morning,
Saw a boy knocked from his seat.
He remembered the lesson that Matthew learned,
And helped the boy to his feet.

"STOP" said Charlie.
"He's no different than me or you.
The same heart that beats inside of you,
Beats inside him, too."

The team beat O'Dea Middle School,
38 to zero.
They carried the boys on their shoulders,
To honor them as heroes.

*Courage for Charlie*

Take the time to know each other.
Is the message we proclaim.
Have the courage to stand for what's right.
And treat everyone the same.

So as you wake for school this morning,
And another day begins.
Remember every person matters,
And courage always wins.

# A message from the author

*My hope for creating this book is that it can help every child who is bullied. We need to put an end to the increasing rate of suicide in our youth due to bullying. It is the leading cause of death for adolescents between the ages of nine and fourteen. Society needs to come together and fix this problem. Our youth are crying out for help. What are we going to do about it. We can no longer pretend it's not happening. It's happening every single day. 123 times a day it happens. That is 123 times too many. Please stand with me and help me make a change. I know we can do it.*

*Love,*

*Beca*

# Acknowledgements

*I would first like to thank my mom and dad for all of their guidance, love and support. I am forever grateful to both of you.*

*To the wonderful city of Bothell, WA: This has been such a wonderful journey and I am continuously humbled by the love and support this city shows me. It truly takes a village. Thank you for being my village.*

*To Coach Bainter and the entire Bothell HS Football organization: Thank you for being my inspiration behind Matthew's character. I can't put into words how much I appreciate you all. Go Cougs!*

*To my amazing publisher/co-author/dear friend, Todd: Your friendship means more to me than you will ever know. Thank you for taking a leap of faith with me.*

*To Jason, my artist: Thank you for bringing the book to life and dealing with me. I appreciate you so much.*

*To my City on a Hill family: Thank you for being a part of my faith journey. From day one, I have been embraced by so much love and acceptance. Thank you for finding me.*

*To my dearest friend Willy: Thank you for showing me a truly genuine and unconditional friendship. I am forever grateful you came into my life. I will always be here for you, buddy!*

*To my greatest joy, Bella: Thank you for all your patience and understanding. I know it's not easy at times with my busy schedule, but your support and love keep me going. There is no one I would rather go through this with. Mommy loves you so much, Angel.*

Made in the USA
San Bernardino, CA
03 December 2018